Go Away, Dark Night

BY LIZ CURTIS HIGGS

Illustrated by Nancy Munger

WATERBROOK
PRESS

COLORADO SPRINGS

Go Away, Dark Night
Published by WaterBrook Press
5446 North Academy Boulevard, Suite 200
Colorado Springs, CO 80918
A division of Bantam Doubleday Dell Publishing Group, Inc.

Scriptures in this book are quoted from
the *International Children's Bible, New Century Version,*
copyright © 1986, 1988 by Word Publishing.
Used by permission.

ISBN 1-57856-129-9

Printed in the United States of America
1998—First Edition

10 9 8 7 6 5 4 3 2 1

For anyone who has ever been afraid.

He called you out of darkness

into his wonderful light.

1 PETER 2:9

Griffin liked lots of things.
He liked Ringo the dog,
Whiskers the cat,
Brownie the horse,
and Larry the goldfish.

But one thing Griffin
did not like at all...

Griffin did not like nighttime.
Griffin was afraid of the dark.

It made his toes curl up
and his hands grow cold
and his heart beat fast
and his legs turn to jelly.
Griffin and darkness
did not get along.
No, not even a little.

I am scared and shaking.

PSALM 55:5

When nighttime came
and the sun disappeared,
when faraway stars
twinkled in the black sky,
Griffin tiptoed around his bedroom
and turned on every single light.
Flick! Snap! Click!

"Now then!" Griffin said as he squeezed his giant,
stuffed bear. "No need to be afraid, Teddy Boy.
See how bright the room is?"

With his brown eyes shut tight,
Griffin pretended he was a bear
like Teddy Boy, all curled up
for a long, wintry nap.

The darkness of the night was just beginning.

PROVERBS 7:9

"Gri-i-i-ffin! Lights out, young man."
His mother's voice floated up the steps
to his bedroom.

His eyes flew open, and his voice
made a froggy croak. "Yes, Mama."

Griffin said *yes*, but he meant *no!*

He would have to check the closet
and peek under the bed
and turn out the lights,
all by himself.

Flick! The overhead bulb went black.

Snap! The corner light by the closet
        turned to shadows.

Click! The lamp on his nightstand
        swallowed the last bite of light.

Griffin's room was as dark as a starless sky
or the forest at midnight
or the inside of a shoebox with the lid on tight.

He hid under his covers,
shivering so fiercely
he was certain his mother
would hear his bones rattling
all the way downstairs.

*I am worried, and I am shaking....My pleasant evening
has become a night of fear.*

ISAIAH 21:4

Griffin dreaded bedtime.

If only Ringo would sleep at his feet
or Whiskers could curl up by his pillow.

His mother shook her head.
"They're outside animals, dear,
and outside they must stay."

"Hoot! Hoot!" called the owl outside.
"Help! Help!" Griffin whispered inside,
trembling under his blankets.

Even his animal friends couldn't
chase away his fear.

If only he could have a *real* friend over,
someone funny and clever,
someone who was not afraid of the dark.
No, not even a little.

But when his neighbor Peter
came to spend the night,
Peter only laughed at Griffin.
"Scaredy-cat!" he taunted and teased.
"Silly you, to be so afraid.
I'm telling! I'm telling!"

Griffin was more discouraged than ever.

A man's friends should be kind to him when he is in trouble.

JOB 6:14

If only somebody *BIG*
would stay with him,
someone brave and strong
and not afraid of anything.

"Mama?" Griffin swallowed the
lump in his throat. "Could
someone big stay in my room tonight?"

"Someone big? In your room?"
She looked surprised. "Why, Griff?"

Griffin's voice was so soft she had to
bend over to hear him. His throat
was full of tears. "I'm scared of the
dark, Mama."

*The greatest person in the kingdom of heaven is the one
who makes himself humble like this child.*

MATTHEW 18:4

She hugged him tight.
"I know just the one to ask,
someone very big indeed."

"You?" Griffin asked.

His mother smiled and shook her head.

"Daddy?"

She shook her head again and her smile grew wider.

Griffin thought hard. "Grandpa?"

This time she laughed. "Bigger
than him! Bigger than all of us!"

His mother whispered one word in his ear.
Griffin's eyes grew as round as dinner plates.

"God?!" Griffin's mouth made a wide O.
"Can God fit in my bedroom?"

"God can fit in your room,
fit in your bed,
fit in *you!*"

I am the Lord your God. I am holding your right hand.
And I tell you, "Don't be afraid.
I will help you."

ISAIAH 41:13

"Is God scared of the dark?"

"Oh, no!" Griffin's mother assured him.
"God isn't scared of anything,
but especially not the dark."

*God is light and in him
there is no darkness at all.*

1 JOHN 1:5

"But I can't see God.
How will I know he's there?"

His mother's smile was as
dazzling as daylight. "That's easy.
You won't be afraid anymore!"

Where God's love is, there is no fear,
because God's perfect love takes away fear.

1 JOHN 4:18

It must be true.
Mothers know these things.

God can be outside and inside.
God is a true friend
who would never tease him.
God is even bigger than Grandpa.

And God isn't afraid of the dark.
No, not even a little!

*I will not be afraid
because the Lord is with me.*

PSALM 118:6

Nighttime sneaked up on Griffin again,
but this time he was ready.

He put on his favorite pajamas,
pulled Teddy Boy out of his toy box,
and folded back the bedcovers with a smile.

"Here we go, God," he sang out,
tiptoeing toward the switch on the wall.

Flick! The overhead bulb went black.

Snap! The corner light by the closet
turned to shadows.

Click! The lamp on his nightstand
swallowed the last bite of light.

Griffin's voice was so-o-o small.
"God? Are you still there?"

God must be there,
because Griffin's fear was *gone*.
So were the shivers and the shakes
and the quivers and the quakes.

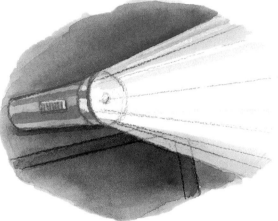

He dove under the bedcovers
and hugged Teddy Boy tight.
"I'm not scared," he boasted
to the bear. "Are you?"

The darkness filled his room, but
Griffin wasn't afraid. No, not even a little.

God is bigger than the darkness.

*The Light shines in the darkness. And the darkness
has not overpowered the Light.*

JOHN 1:5

It wasn't long before his mother's voice
floated up the steps and into his bedroom.

"How are you doing, Griff?"

But Griffin didn't hear his mother.
He didn't hear Ringo barking at the moon
or Whiskers meowing on the porch
or the wise old owl hooting in the tree.

Griffin was fast asleep.

I go to bed and sleep in peace.
Lord, only you keep me safe.

PSALM 4:8

The last thing Griffin remembered
before his waking had turned to sleeping
was a strong, yet gentle, voice,
whispering like the night wind:

Put away your fears, my child.
Give them all to me.
Love will keep you safe this night.
Sleep tight, child. Sleep tight.

The Lord is my light and the one who saves me.
I fear no one.

PSALM 27:1